Makayla Cares about Others

Virginia Kroll

illustrated by **Nancy Cote**

Albert Whitman & Company, Morton Grove, Illinois

The Way I Act Books:

Cristina Keeps a Promise • *Forgiving a Friend* • *Good Neighbor Nicholas*
Honest Ashley • *Jason Takes Responsibility* • *Makayla Cares about Others* • *Ryan Respects*

The Way I Feel Books:

When I Care about Others • *When I Feel Angry*
When I Feel Good about Myself • *When I Feel Jealous*
When I Feel Sad • *When I Feel Scared* • *When I Miss You*

Library of Congress Cataloging-in-Publication Data

Kroll, Virginia L.
Makayla cares about others / by Virginia Kroll ; illustrated by Nancy Cote.
p. cm.
Summary: With her tool box and her talent for fixing things, eight-year-old Makayla tries to mend a neighbor's broken heart.
ISBN 13: 978-0-8075-4945-2 (hardcover)
[1. Helpfulness—Fiction. 2. Neighborliness—Fiction.] I. Cote, Nancy, ill. II. Title.
PZ7.K9227Mak 2007 [E]—dc22 2006023400

The design is by Carol Gildar.
For more information about Albert Whitman & Company, please visit our web site at www.albertwhitman.com.

Lovingly to Trish Pecuch and Andi Hummel,
a pair of caring friends.—v.k.

To Jill, an endless source of pride and joy, who
truly knows the meaning of caring.—n.c.

Makayla was good with her hands. Whenever something broke, she was ready to mend it. So Grandpa gave her a toolbox that she took wherever she went.

She glued Aunt Karen's broken clay turtle.

She hammered Mr. Bell's bird feeder back into place and clipped the broken branch off Miss Barbati's blueberry bush.

She even measured baby blankets for the Nicotera twins to see how much fabric Mom would need to finish them.

One summer Monday morning, Makayla was walking to Grandpa's when she noticed her next-door neighbor starting a new flower bed. "Hi, Mrs. MacFee," Makayla called. She saw Mrs. MacFee swipe at some tears.

"What's wrong?" Makayla asked.

"Furgus died over the weekend while you and your family were away at your aunt and uncle's," said Mrs. MacFee. She heaved a huge sigh. "I'm planting a memory garden in his honor."

"Oh, no!" Makayla cried. She had loved the smoky-gray cat that had found his way onto Mrs. MacFee's porch during a thick fog sixteen years ago. That was eight whole years before Makayla was even born.

He always meowed a hearty "hello" when he stretched out on the stoop to soak up some sunshine, and he purred whenever Makayla petted his fluffy fur. Mrs. MacFee and Makayla called him "Flower Face" because he liked to lie flat among the blooms. All you could see was his face peeking out.

Makayla's eyes filled with tears.

Mrs. MacFee patted down a newly planted snapdragon and struggled to stand up. "Whew! That's hard on my knees."

Makayla knew she should help. She cared about Mrs. MacFee and Furgus, after all. But she had a huge problem. She was absolutely, positively terrified of bugs! And there were bugs in that dirt for sure!

Bees and flies made her shriek. Last summer when she was digging in Grandpa's garden, a centipede had scurried right over her flip-flopped foot.

As if that wasn't bad enough, Makayla had found an earwig wriggling in the cuff of her pants at bathtime that very same day. She shivered just thinking about those bugs. No more digging for her! Makayla went home right away. She even forgot her toolbox.

Back in her room, Makayla tried playing with her toy horse collection. But she kept going to the window to watch Mrs. MacFee in her garden.

Suddenly Makayla remembered something. Grandpa couldn't eat sweets anymore, but he still took Makayla to their favorite ice cream place. Makayla knew he'd love a sugar cone of orange sherbet with a zillion chocolate sprinkles, but he always just sipped ice water while she had her treat. One day she asked him, "Why do we still come here if you can't enjoy it?"

"Because *you* can," he had said, playfully pinching her nose. And Makayla remembered thinking, *Now I know what caring means—doing things for other people, even when you don't have to and when it's hard to do.*

Makayla went back to Mrs. MacFee's. She squeezed her eyes shut and took a deep breath. "I'll help you, Mrs. MacFee," she said. "I'll dig, and you plant, okay? It'll get done faster that way." She took the spade from her neighbor's hands.

Makayla dug fast. She saw a few earthworms squiggling and a shiny beetle or two. She kept focusing on something else Grandpa had said: "Those little critters are more afraid of you than you are of them." Soon the job was finished.

Mrs. MacFee sniffled and glanced at Makayla's toolbox. "I feel like my heart is breaking. It sure could use some fixing," she said.

Some fixing? Makayla thought. *How do you fix a broken heart? Ruler? Glue? Don't think so. Duct tape? Hammer? Clippers? No way! Screwdriver? Ruler? Spade? Nope.* This time, Makayla didn't need any tools to be helpful.

She opened her arms and wrapped them around Mrs. MacFee. "I'm so sorry about Furgus," she said, giving her neighbor a warm, tight hug.

She and Mrs. MacFee sat down on Furgus's favorite step. They talked about Furgus for a long time. "He was a very special cat. I'll miss him, too," Makayla said.

"Thank you for everything, Makayla dear," said Mrs. MacFee. "I think my heart is mending already. And Furgus would love those flowers!"

"Yes, he would," said Makayla. "Well, Grandpa's expecting me."

Mrs. MacFee smiled. Makayla smiled back.

When Makayla got to Grandpa's, she told him about Furgus and asked, "Grandpa, will you help me make a marker for his memory garden?"

"I sure will," Grandpa said.

"Thanks, Grandpa. What needs to be done today?" Makayla asked.

"Well," Grandpa said, "I was going to weed the garden, but . . ."

MAKAYLA

Makayla interrupted. "I'll help you," she said.

Grandpa smiled at the surprise. "There might be a bug or two in that dirt," he said.

"That's okay, Grandpa."

Makayla thought about caring again. And she and Grandpa set to weeding his garden—wrigglers, squigglers, and all.